Robin Muller

13 Ghosts
of Halloween

illustrated by
Patricia Storms

Scholastic Canada Ltd.

New York Toronto London Auckland Sydney
Mexico City New Delhi Hong Kong Buenos Aires

To Khalen Perkins, with howls
and shrieks and candy
bags full of Happy Halloween.
— R.M.

For my Guido.
— P.S.

Scholastic Canada Ltd.
604 King Street West, Toronto, Ontario M5V 1E1, Canada

Scholastic Inc.
557 Broadway, New York, NY 10012, USA

Scholastic Australia Pty Limited
PO Box 579, Gosford, NSW 2250, Australia

Scholastic New Zealand Limited
Private Bag 94407, Greenmount, Auckland, New Zealand

Scholastic Children's Books
Euston House, 24 Eversholt Street, London NW1 1DB, UK

The illustrations in this book were created digitally.
The type is set in 20 point Korinna.

Library and Archives Canada Cataloguing in Publication
Muller, Robin
13 ghosts of Halloween / Robin Muller ; illustrations by Patricia Storms.
ISBN 978-0-439-93569-2

I. Storms, Patricia II. Title. III. Title: Thirteen ghosts of Halloween.
PS8576.U424T44 2007   jC813'.54   C2006-906673-6

6 5 4 3 2 1   Printed in Singapore   07 08 09 10 11

On the first stroke of midnight
Oh, nothing frightens me!
Not a vulture in a dead tree.

On the second stroke of midnight
Oh, nothing frightens me!
Not two shrunken heads
Or a vulture in a dead tree.

On the third stroke of midnight
Oh, nothing frightens me!
Not three black cats
Two shrunken heads
Or a vulture in a dead tree.

On the fourth stroke of midnight
Oh, nothing frightens me!
Not four darting bats
Three black cats
Two shrunken heads
Or a vulture in a dead tree.

On the fifth stroke of midnight
No, nothing frightens me!
Not five bogeymen

Four darting bats
Three black cats
Two shrunken heads
Or a vulture in a dead tree.

On the sixth stroke of midnight
Oh, nothing frightens me!
Not six pumpkins grinning
Five bogeymen

Four darting bats
Three black cats
Two shrunken heads
Or a vulture in a dead tree.

On the seventh stroke of midnight
Oh, nothing frightens me!
Not seven spiders spinning
Six pumpkins grinning
Five bogeymen
Four darting bats
Three black cats
Two shrunken heads
Or a vulture in a dead tree.

On the eighth stroke of midnight
Oh, nothing frightens me!
Not eight mummies moaning
Seven spiders spinning
Six pumpkins grinning
Five bogeymen
Four darting bats
Three black cats
Two shrunken heads
Or a vulture in a dead tree.

On the ninth stroke of midnight
Oh, nothing frightens me!
Not nine witches cackling
Eight mummies moaning
Seven spiders spinning
Six pumpkins grinning
Five bogeymen

Four darting bats
Three black cats
Two shrunken heads
Or a vulture in a dead tree.

On the tenth stroke of midnight
Oh, nothing frightens me!
Not ten werewolves howling
Nine witches cackling
Eight mummies moaning
Seven spiders spinning
Six pumpkins grinning
Five bogeymen

Four darting bats
Three black cats
Two shrunken heads
Or a vulture in a dead tree.

On the eleventh stroke of midnight

Oh, nothing frightens me!

Not eleven goblins giggling

Ten werewolves howling

Nine witches cackling

Eight mummies moaning

Seven spiders spinning

Six pumpkins grinning

Five bogeymen

Four darting bats

Three black cats

Two shrunken heads

Or a vulture in a dead tree.

On the twelfth stroke of midnight
Oh, nothing frightens me!
Not twelve vampires rising
Eleven goblins giggling
Ten werewolves howling
Nine witches cackling
Eight mummies moaning
Seven spiders spinning
Six pumpkins grinning
Five bogeymen
Four darting bats
Three black cats
Two shrunken heads
Or a vulture in a dead tree.

On the **thirteenth** stroke of midnight

Yes, something frightened me . . .